DEDICATED TO MY DAD, WHO SHOWED ME
HOW TO LIVE IN the LIGHT.
— ALBERT

TO ALL the STARS THAT LIT ME
ON MY JOURNEY.
— FLAVIA

bala
kids

Bala Kids
An imprint of Shambhala Publications, Inc.
4720 Walnut Street
Boulder, Colorado 80301
www.shambhala.com

Text © 2021 by Albert Strasser
Illustrations © 2021 by Flavia Sorrentino

Design by Kara Plikaitis

9 8 7 6 5 4 3 2 1

First Edition
Printed in China

⊗This edition is printed on acid-free paper that meets the American National Standards Institute Z39.48 Standard.
♻Shambhala Publications makes every effort to print on recycled paper. For more information please visit www.shambhala.com.
Bala Kids is distributed worldwide by Penguin Random House, Inc., and its subsidiaries.

Library of Congress Cataloging-in-Publication Data
Names: Strasser, Albert, author. | Sorrentino, Flavia, illustrator.
Title: Afraid of the light: a story about facing your fears / Albert
   Strasser; illustrated by Flavia Sorrentino.
Description: First edition. | Boulder, Colorado: Bala Kids, 2021. |
   Audience: Ages 4–8. | Summary: In order to find his missing shoe, Ditter
   von Dapp must first confront his fear of the light and illuminate his
   dark cave dwelling.
Identifiers: LCCN 2019052980 | ISBN 9781611808148 (hardback)
Subjects: CYAC: Stories in rhyme. | Fear—Fiction.
Classification: LCC PZ8.3.S8974 Af 2021 | DDC [E]—dc23
LC record available at https://lccn.loc.gov/2019052980

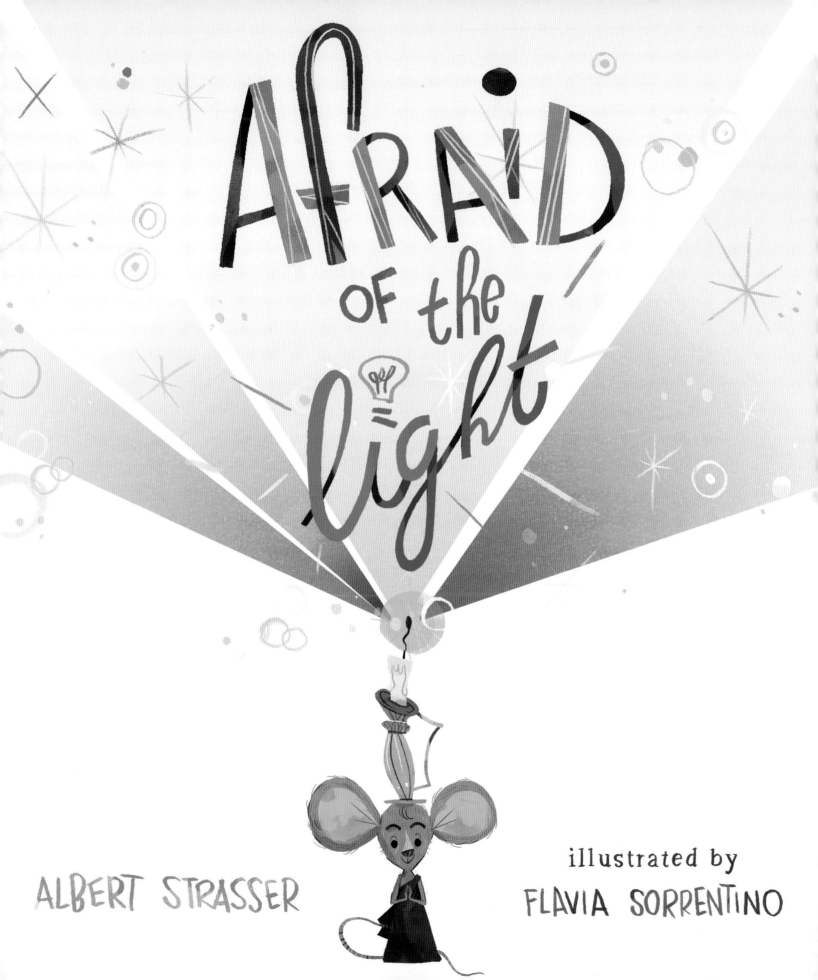

Afraid of the light

ALBERT STRASSER

illustrated by
FLAVIA SORRENTINO

There once was a chap called Ditter von Dapp
who lived deep inside of a cave.

He couldn't stand sunlight—"It's too blinding and bright!"—
so always he stayed in the shade.

He never used candles or even a flashlight.
He never used anything the slightest bit bright.
He kept all these things in a chest out of sight

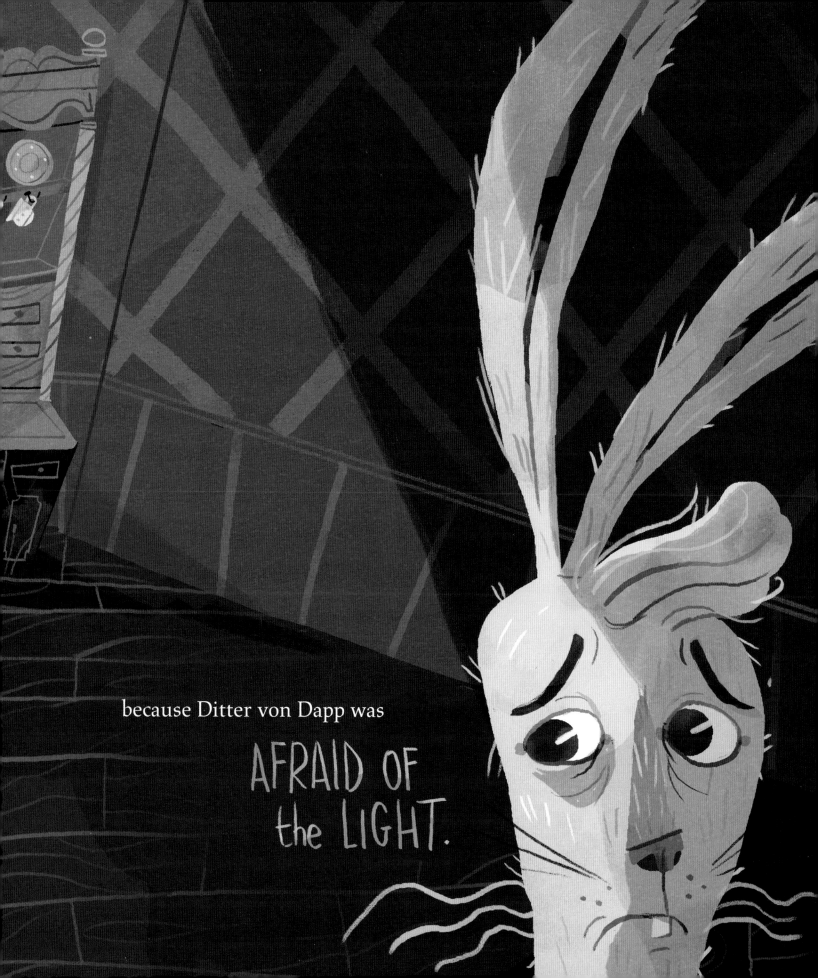

because Ditter von Dapp was

AFRAID OF
the LIGHT.

"People tell me they're afraid of the dark,
and to that I just laugh, har har har!
What could be scary when there's nothing to see?
The dark isn't scary—it's the light that scares me!

"It could blind me, unwind me, it could drive me insane!
Or illuminate things I don't like.
Much better to stay in the cozy, dim dark
than risk being caught in the light."

Of course, in the dark, even he would remark,
"It's a bit hard to see what's around.
But better to stick with the dark, which I know,
than in the light be found."

So squinting he'd scuttle and shuffle and slip
and shlalop and shloof and stumble and trip

from his bed to his kitchen and his living room, too.
He stayed in the dark, for that's what he knew.

But then one day as he put on his socks,
he found with dismay, "My left shoe has been lost!
I can't walk around with only one shoe!
My toes will get cold! Oh garfunkle-ka-poo!"

He looked high and low.
He looked left and right.
He looked all day
and he looked all night.

The trouble, of course, is that looking is tough.
When you're looking in darkness—all you see is dark stuff.
"Ah, ker-snuff-it!" he grumpily said.
"I guess I'll have to try something new instead."

With a frown on his face, he opened the chest
where he kept all his candles and lights.
He pulled out a candle and pulled out a match
and carefully squinted his eyes.

As he lit up the match, and the candlewick, too,
he cautiously opened his eyes.
And what he discovered, although a bit scary,
was a wonderful surprise!

It didn't blind him, unwind him, or drive him insane.
In fact, it was quite a treat!
The light: it lit the shadows.
The flame: it made some heat.

Looking around at his dingy old cave,
he was thrilled with what was there:
beautiful colors and shapes and textures.
"I can't believe I was scared!

"But I mustn't get carried away or forget
what I lit this candle to find.
I've got to keep searching for my missing left shoe,
now that I'm not quite so blind."

So he searched and he sought and he looked all around,
but his gosh-darn left shoe just could not be found.
"One candle won't do," he said with a frown.
"I need some more light."
So with a leap and a bound . . .

. . . he frolicked and gleefully lit all his lights.
He jumped and he hollered and he yelled with delight

as he looked at his cave that was
gleaming with light,
everything illuminated, twinkling
and bright.

In just 49 minutes his whole cave had been lit
with 108 candles, and that wasn't it!
There were kerosene lamps and a chandelier, too.
Every inch of his cave glowed a warm golden hue.

And that's when he saw, from the corner of his eye,
a little mouse in red robes who was standing nearby.
She smiled and slowly stepped to the side
to reveal his left shoe—oh, what a surprise!

"It was you all along!" he said with a laugh,
as he realized this mouse had provided a path.
She had not taken his shoe simply for play.
She'd taken the shoe to show Von Dapp the way.

"All this time, my dear mouse, I've been afraid of the light.
I lived in the dark. It was always like night.
But now I see clearly what's actually true:
what I feared, in fact, was that which was new.

"The darkness, you see, was familiar to me,
so in my mind I made light a feared enemy.
I thought up long stories about what it could do,
how it might drive me crazy or turn me to goo.

"But now thanks to you taking my gosh-darn left shoe
I see that my thinking was simply untrue.
There's no reason at all to be afraid of the light.
Oh goodness, oh golly—what a delight!"

So, my dears, the next time you can't find your shoe, or you're stuck and just not sure what to do,

here is my tidbit of insight for you:

SIMPLY, COURAGEOUSLY, FEARLESSLY, TRY SOMETHING NEW.

AUTHOR'S NOTE

Sometimes I think, "I wish all my problems would just go away. Then I would never have to feel uncomfortable or afraid!" But things often simply do not go the way we hope or plan. Whether it be a broken toy, someone calling you a mean name, or a missing left shoe, life's many challenges never stop showing up.

But there is good news! Imagine if Von Dapp's shoe had never gone missing—he'd still be living in the dark! In the same way, life's surprises (which we normally call "problems") may actually be gifts. They can lead us to view the world, and even ourselves, in new and exciting ways.

The idea for this story came from a very old book with a very creepy title: *The Tibetan Book of the Dead*. With a name like that, you may be surprised to hear that it's a book about discovering joy—not mummies or ghosts. It teaches that well-being is found by taking small, courageous steps out of our familiar worlds (which can sometimes feel like dark caves) and into the bright lights of the unknown.

May this tall tale be an inspiration to all: to lean into fear, to try something new, and to step bravely into the light.